姬兒和豆萃

Jill and the Beanstalk

by Manju Gregory
illustrated by David Anstey

Chinese translation by Sylvia Denham

mantra

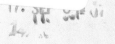

傑克和她的妹妹爬山，
傑克摔倒了，現在臥病在家，
他們沒有東西吃，覺得很可憐，
要是巨人沒有把他們的爸爸吞噬就好了。

Jack climbed a hill with his sister Jill.
Jack fell down and now he's ill.
There's nothing to eat, they're feeling sad,
If only the Giant hadn't swallowed their dad.

媽媽問姬兒道：「你有沒有想過
可以賣了我們的牛來籌錢啊？」

Mum asked Jill, "Do you think somehow
You could raise money selling our cow?"

姫兒行了不足一里，便遇到一個男人在梯欄旁邊。
「用這些豆跟你交換那隻牛，」他說。
「豆！」姫兒叫道，「你發神經嗎？」
那個男人解釋道：「這些是神奇的豆，它們會為你帶來你從未見過的禮物。」

Jill had barely walked a mile when she met a man beside a stile.
"Swap you these beans for that cow," he said.
"Beans!" cried Jill. "Are you off your head?"
The man explained, "These are magic beans. They bring you gifts you've never seen."

姫兒拿它們回家給媽媽看，
媽媽大聲叫道：「我早就應該讓我得兒子去！」
她把豆扔向姫兒的腳，
更要她餓著肚子上床去。

Jill took them home to show her mum
Who cried out loud, "I should have sent my son!"
She threw the beans down at Jill's feet
And sent her to bed with nothing to eat.

早睡早起，姬兒晨早醒來便看到出乎意料的驚奇，
一棵豆莖一直生長到天空中去。
姬兒緊抱著莖葉，抓著豆其，
爬上這棵隨風飄蕩的大豆莖。

Early to bed, early to rise,
Jill woke up at dawn with a mighty surprise.
A beanstalk had grown right up to the skies.
Catching hold of the stalk, clinging fast to the leaves,
She climbed the great plant as it swayed in the breeze.

姬兒聽到叫喊聲，那是她的媽媽啊！
「立刻下來，照顧你的哥哥啊！」
但姬兒繼續爬， 她沒有停，
一直向上去，直到豆莖的尖頂。

Jill heard a shout, it was her mother!
"Come down at once, look after your brother!"
But Jill just kept on climbing, she didn't stop,
All the way upwards, right to the top.

她跳下豆莖，聽到很大的哭聲，
一個小女孩哭著說：「我的羊兒在那裏？
牠們趁我睡覺時溜走了。」
「我在那裏？」姬兒問道。

She leapt off the beanstalk, and heard a loud weep.
A little girl cried, "Oh, where are my sheep?
They've wandered away while I was asleep."
"Where am I?" asked Jill.

「你在巨人居住得地方，
你是來報仇抑或時來寬恕的呢？
現在讓我將曲杖一揮，你便選擇你的命運吧，
爬落豆莖抑或繼續前往巨人的大門口？」

"You're in the land where the Giant lives.
Did you come to avenge or come to forgive?
With a wave of my crook now choose your fate,
Back down the beanstalk or onto the Giant's Gate?"

姫兒站在巨人的屋前，
覺得很渺小，害怕得像一隻顫抖的小鼠。
一個怪異的老婦站在一旁，
將蜘蛛網從空中掃去，
「小女孩，你爲什麼在這裡？爲什麼啊？爲什麼？

Jill stood in front of the Giant's house
Feeling tiny and scared like a quivering mouse.
A strange old woman was standing by,
Brushing cobwebs out of the sky.
"Little girl, why are you here? Why, oh why?"

當她正在說話時，地面開始搖動，發出震耳欲聾的聲音，好像大地震一樣。
那老婦說：「快快走進去，只有一個地方你可以躲藏的...躲進烤爐內！
如果你不想死的話，便要像雪一樣的沉靜，一口氣也不要吸，切勿嘆氣。」

As she spoke the ground began to shake, with a deafening sound like a mighty earthquake.
The woman said, "Quick run inside. There's only one place...in the oven you'll hide!
Take barely one breath, don't utter a sigh, stay silent as snow, if you don't want to die."

姫兒蹲縮在烤爐內，她做錯了什麼？她是多麼的想在家中與媽媽一起啊。

巨人說：「菲，費，弗，分。我聞到地球人的血腥味。」

「丈夫啊，你只是聞到我烤的餡餅內的雀肉而已，總共二十四隻畫眉鳥都從天空跌了下來。」

Jill crouched in the oven. What had she done? How she wished she were home with her mum.

The Giant spoke, "Fee, fi, faw, fum. I smell the blood of an earthly man."

"Husband, you smell only the birds I baked in a pie. All four and twenty dropped out of the sky."

巨人咆哮道：「我對你那些細小的菜式全無興趣，
妻子啊，我需要吃東西，快到廚房拿肉給我吃！」
從烤爐門的隙縫處，姬兒看到巨人吞吃了一隻野豬。

The Giant bawled, "I have no wish to even try your dainty dish.
Wife, I need to eat. Go to the kitchen and fetch me my meat!"
From a gap in the oven door, Jill watched the Giant devour a wild boar.

巨人往椅後靠，一點也不高興，
他大聲吼叫：「拿我的鵝來，快呀！」
他閉上眼睛說：「鵝遞送！」
鵝便立刻生下一枚光亮的金蛋，令姬兒十分驚訝。
巨人很高興，
數著一隻又一隻的純金蛋。
跟著巨人便睡著了，更開始打鼾，
聲音巨大如獅吼！

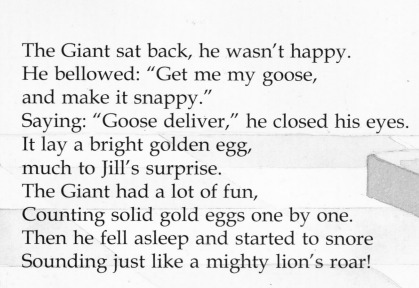

The Giant sat back, he wasn't happy.
He bellowed: "Get me my goose,
and make it snappy."
Saying: "Goose deliver," he closed his eyes.
It lay a bright golden egg,
much to Jill's surprise.
The Giant had a lot of fun,
Counting solid gold eggs one by one.
Then he fell asleep and started to snore
Sounding just like a mighty lion's roar!

姬兒知道她可以在巨人睡覺時逃走，
於是便小心地從烤爐爬出來。
她想起她的朋友湯姆的經驗，
他偷了一隻豬後便快快逃走。
於是她便緊緊抓住那隻鵝，一直的跑。
「我一定要盡快走到那棵豆莖處。」

Jill knew she could escape while the Giant slept.
So carefully out of the oven she crept.
Then she remembered what her friend, Tom, had done.
Stole a pig and away he'd run.
Grabbing the goose, she ran and ran.
"I must get to that beanstalk as fast as I can."

她從豆莖滑下，大聲叫道：「我回來了！」
媽媽和傑克立即從屋中走出來。

She slid down the stalk shouting, "I'm back!"
And out of the house came mother and Jack.

「你的哥哥和我都很擔心，你怎樣沿豆莖爬上天空的？」
「但是媽媽啊，」姬兒說，「我沒事呀，你們看我的手上有什麼。」
「鵝遞送，」姬兒重復地說巨人說的幾個字，
鵝便立刻生下一隻光亮的金蛋。

"We've been worried sick, your brother and I. How could you climb that great stalk to the sky?"
"But Mum," Jill said, "I came to no harm. And look what I have under my arm."
"Goose deliver," Jill repeated the words that the Giant had said,
And the goose instantly laid a bright golden egg.

姬兒這次造訪巨人的家，令她的一家人都不用再捱餓和感到絕望。

Jill's visit to the Giant's lair kept her family from hunger and despair.

傑克難免對妹妹姬兒感到羨慕，
他希望他不是去了爬山，而是去了爬豆莖。
他誇張得很，並經常說
如果他遇到那巨人，他必定會砍下他的頭。

Jack couldn't help feeling envious of his sister Jill.
He wished he'd climbed a beanstalk instead of a hill.
Jack boasted a lot and often said
If he'd met the Giant he would've chopped off his head.

他們的媽媽警告他們不要去爬豆莖，
但姬兒對傑克的空談廢話感到很不耐煩。
有一天，姬兒經過聰明的改裝後，沿豆莖
爬上天空去。

Their mother had warned them not to climb that stalk
But Jill was fed up with Jack's idle talk.
One day, in clever disguise, Jill climbed up the beanstalk
And reached the skies.

那名老婦在大門旁邊坐著，看來很憂傷，
巨人對她很兇惡，很刻薄。
自從他的鵝被偷走後，
他變得日益可怕。

The old woman sat by the gate looking sad,
The evil Giant treated her bad, very bad.
He'd become more gruesome by the day,
Since his goose had been stolen away.

巨人的妻子沒有認出姬兒，
但她卻聽到雷鳴一樣的腳步聲從山上傳來。
「是巨人啊！」她叫道，「如果他聞到你的血腥味，他肯定會殺你的。」

The Giant's wife didn't recognise Jill,
But she heard the sound of thundering footsteps coming down the hill.
"The Giant!" she cried. "If he smells your blood now, he's sure to kill."

「嘿克里、嘀克利、哆！
快躲到鐘內去！」

"Hickory dickory dock,
Quick, go hide in the clock!"

「菲，費，弗，分。我聞到地球人的血腥味。
讓他生存抑或讓他死，我會砍下他的頭的，」巨人說。
「你只是聞到我新鮮烤焗的餡餅而已，我向愛心女皇借了一張食譜。」
「我是巨人啊，妻子，我需要吃東西，快到廚房拿肉給我吃。」

"Fe fi faw fum, I smell the blood of an earthly man.
Let him be alive or let him be dead, I'll chop off his head," the Giant said.
"You smell only my freshly baked tarts, I borrowed a recipe from the Queen of Hearts."
"I'm a Giant, wife, I need to eat. Go to the kitchen and get me my meat."

巨人像上次一樣拼命地吞下動物。
過了一個鐘頭，他又要更多的肉，
他的妻子取來一座豎琴，一座輝煌無比的東西，
用純金造的，並有一百條弦線。
巨人覺得很煩悶，便叫道：「奏樂！」
那豎琴便立即自動奏出音樂來，

The Giant gorged on beast as before.
One full hour passed by, then he called for more.
His wife brought in a harp, the most magnificent of things,
Made out of pure gold with a hundred strings.
The Giant yelled: "Play," he was feeling bored.
The harp instantly played of its own accord.

一首平和甜美的搖籃曲，笨重的巨人很快便睡著了。
姬兒很想要那座自動奏樂的豎琴，她實在很想擁有它啊！
她戰戰兢兢地從鐘內爬出來，趁著巨人熟睡抓住金豎琴。

A lullaby so calm and sweet, the lumbering Giant fell fast asleep.
Jill wanted the harp that played without touch. She wanted it so very much!
Out of the clock she nervously crept, and grabbed the harp of gold whilst the Giant slept.

姫兒向著豆莖一直走，踢到一隻團團轉追著自己尾巴的狗，
當豎琴叫：「主人！主人！」時，巨人醒了，起身追過來，
姫兒知道她要走得更快。

To the beanstalk Jill was bound, tripping over a dog, running round and round.
When the harp cried out: "MASTER! MASTER!" The Giant awoke, got up and ran after.
Jill knew she would have to run faster and faster

巨人怒吼道：「你以爲你可以走！
還記得笛手的兒子湯姆的遭遇吧！」
姬兒緊緊握著豎琴，一直的跑，
「我一定要盡快走到那棵豆莖處。」

The Giant howled, "So you think you can run!
Look what happened to Tom, the piper's son!"
Holding onto the harp, Jill ran and ran,
"I must get to that beanstalk as fast as I can."

她從豆莖滑下，那豎琴叫道：「主人！」
醜陋的巨人雷鳴一樣的跟著追來。
姬兒抓著砍木的斧頭，
盡快將豆莖亂劈。

She slid down the stalk, the harp cried: "MASTER!"
The great ugly Giant came thundering after.
Jill grabbed the axe for cutting wood
And hacked down the beanstalk as fast as she could.

巨人的每一步都令豆莖隆隆地響，而姬兒用斧頭亂劈亦令巨人摔倒，
巨人猛然地向下墮去！
傑克、姬兒和媽媽驚訝地望著巨人摔到地面十尺以下。

Each Giant's step caused the stalk to rumble. Jill's hack of the axe caused the Giant to tumble.
Down down the Giant plunged!
Jack, Jill and mum watched in wonder as the giant CRASHED, ten feet under.

現在傑克、姬兒和他們的媽媽
唱著金豎琴奏出的曲調和歌謠過日子。

Jack, Jill and their mother now spend their days,
Singing songs and rhymes that the golden harp plays.

British Library Cataloguing-in-Publication Data:
a catalogue record for this book is available
from the British Library.

First published 2004 by Mantra
5 Alexandra Grove, London N12 8NU, UK
www.mantralingua.com